Flute

Contents / Inhalt / Sommaire / Inhoud

Track

- ① *Tuning Note A*
- ② ⑫ **Marmalade Mix** 2
- ③ ⑬ **In a Purrsian Market** 3
- ④ ⑭ **Burmese Blue** 4
- ⑤ ⑮ **Bird Cage Stalk** 5
- ⑥ ⑯ **Tortoise-Shell Tango** 6
- ⑦ ⑰ **Tom-Tom** 7
- ⑧ ⑱ **Paws for Thought** 8
- ⑨ ⑲ **Gone Fishin'** 9
- ⑩ ⑳ **Cat-Astrophe** 10
- ⑪ ㉑ **Cats' Eyes** 12

● Accompaniment only / Begleitung (ohne Solostimme) /
Accompagnement (sans la partie solo) / Begeleiding (zonder solopartij)

○ Solo with accompaniment / Solostimme mit Begleitung /
Solo avec accompagnement / Solo met begeleiding

Colin Cowles

Marmalade Mix

Colin Cowles

In a Purrsian Market

Colin Cowles

Poco a poco dim. et Rit.

Burmese Blue

Colin Cowles

Bird Cage Stalk

Colin Cowles

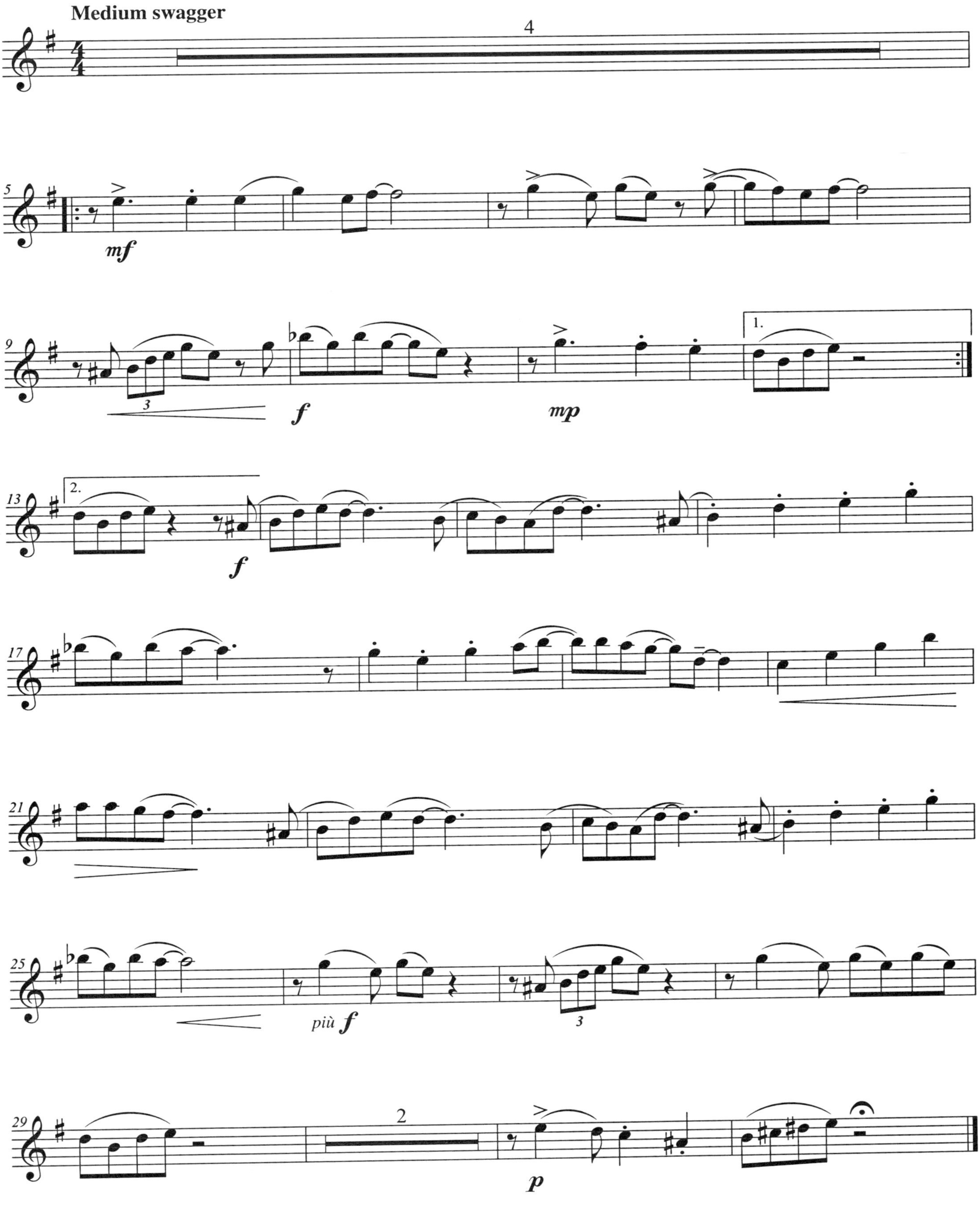

Tortoise-Shell Tango

Colin Cowles

Tom-Tom

Colin Cowles

Paws for Thought

Colin Cowles

Gone Fishin'

Colin Cowles

Cat-Astrophe

Colin Cowles

Flute

Colin Cowles

Fleming Road, Corby, Northants, NN17 4SN

© Copyright 2005 by Fentone Music

All rights reserved. No part of this book may be reproduced in any form, by print, photocopy, microfilm or any other means without written permission of the publisher.

A TAIL OR TWO
Colin Cowles
Flute and Piano
ISMN M-2300-0896-9
Order Number: F 896-400
CD Number: FR 052-3

Printed in the EU

Contents / Inhalt / Sommaire / Inhoud

Track

	Introduction	3
1	*Tuning Note A*	
2 **12**	**Marmalade Mix**	5
3 **13**	**In a Purrsian Market**	8
4 **14**	**Burmese Blue**	11
5 **15**	**Bird Cage Stalk**	14
6 **16**	**Tortoise-Shell Tango**	16
7 **17**	**Tom-Tom**	19
8 **18**	**Paws for Thought**	22
9 **19**	**Gone Fishin'**	26
10 **20**	**Cat-Astrophe**	29
11 **21**	**Cats' Eyes**	34
	Vorwort	37
	Introduction	38
	Introductie	39

● Accompaniment only / Begleitung (ohne Solostimme) / Accompagnement (sans la partie solo) / Begeleiding (zonder solopartij)

○ Solo with accompaniment / Solostimme mit Begleitung / Solo avec accompagnement / Solo met begeleiding

Introduction

As a cat lover it was inevitable that Colin Cowles would compose a set of imaginative pieces about our 'furry friends'. His own cats, Puss, Boo and Olli were important members of the family for some thirty years. These short descriptive pieces are modestly challenging both technically and musically, and as such make ideal teaching and performing material for players of moderate grade. Play them with a sense of humour and bring the individual cats to life!

Colin Cowles

Colin Cowles has made his main career in music education. In the early days he held school posts but he realised that composing was becoming increasingly important to him. He became a peripatetic teacher, a move which also allowed him time to concentrate on composition. He has written a wealth of pieces for those in the early stages of learning an instrument. His compositions cover a wide range of styles, instruments and levels of performing expertise. His sense of humour, which shines through in much of his music, appeals to both teachers and pupils alike although even his most light-hearted works have an underlying seriousness of intent, combining pleasure with learning.

Marmalade Mix

Colin Cowles

Marmalade Mix

Marmalade Mix

3 13

In a Purrsian Market

Colin Cowles

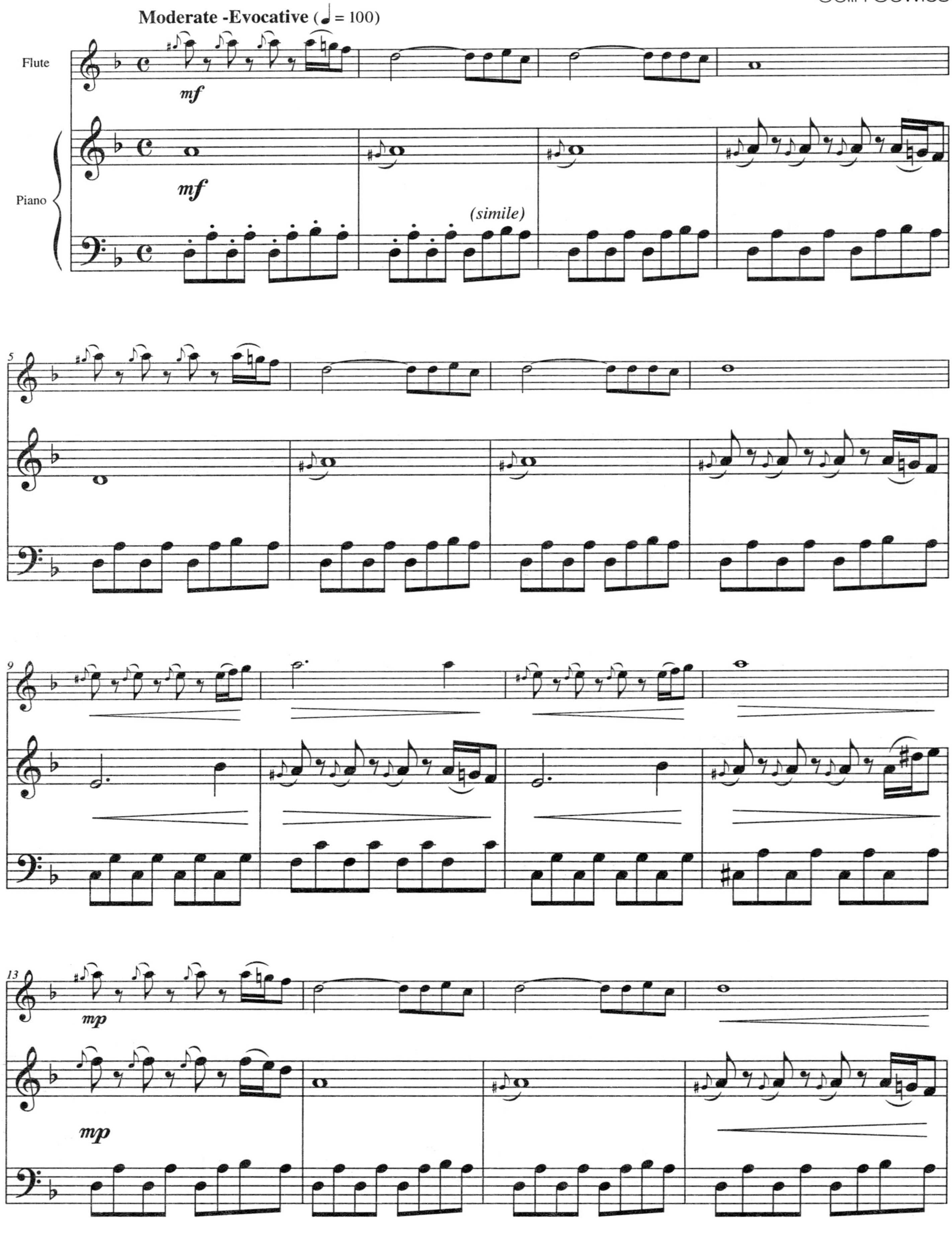
Moderate -Evocative (♩ = 100)
Flute
Piano
mf
mf
(simile)
mp
mp

In a Purrsian Market

In a Purrsian Market

Burmese Blue

Colin Cowles

Burmese Blue

Burmese Blue

Bird Cage Stalk

Colin Cowles

Bird Cage Stalk

Tortoise-Shell Tango

Colin Cowles

Tortoise-Shell Tango

Tortoise-Shell Tango

Tom-Tom

Colin Cowles

Tom-Tom

20

Tom-Tom

Paws for Thought

Colin Cowles

Paws for Thought

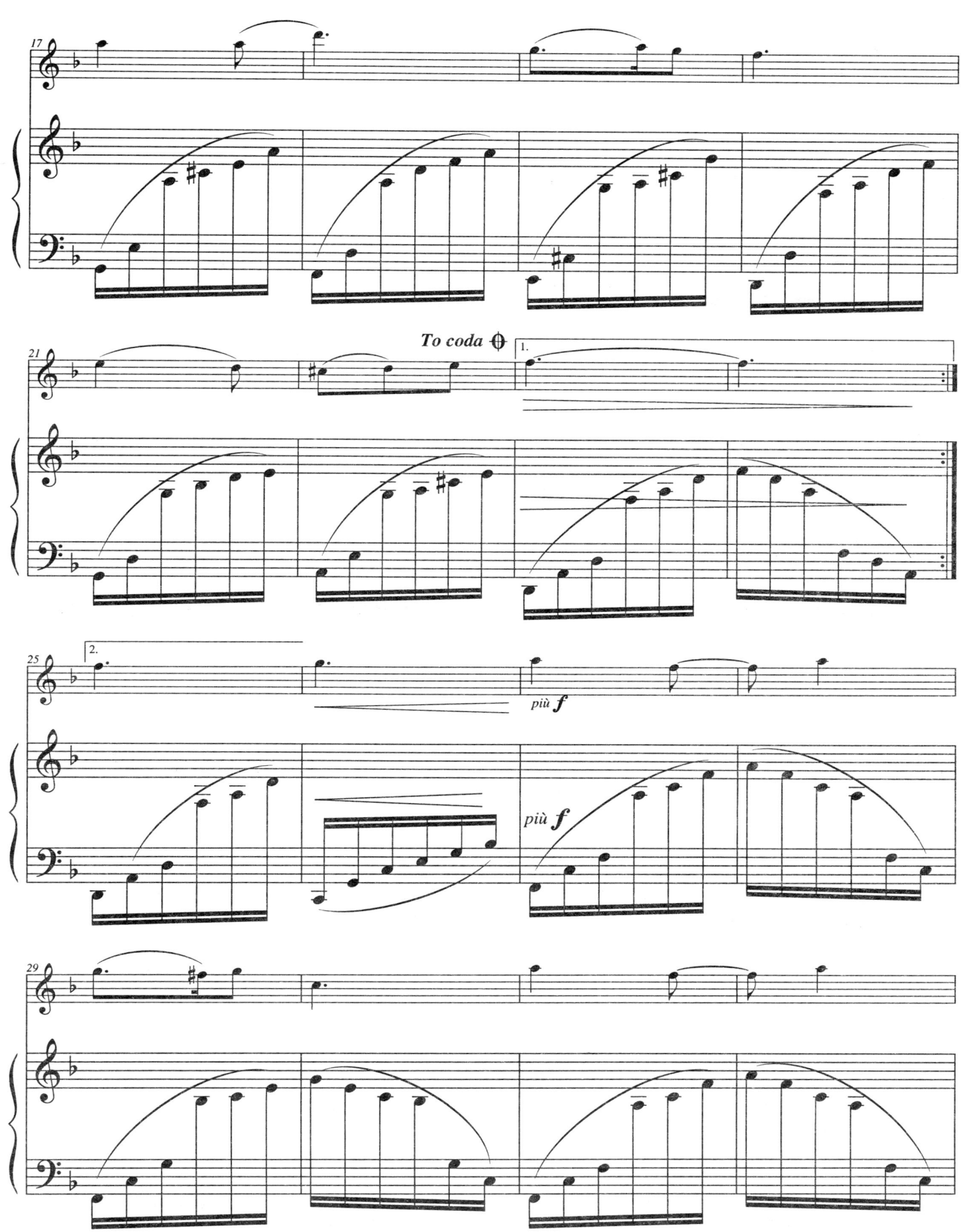

Paws for Thought

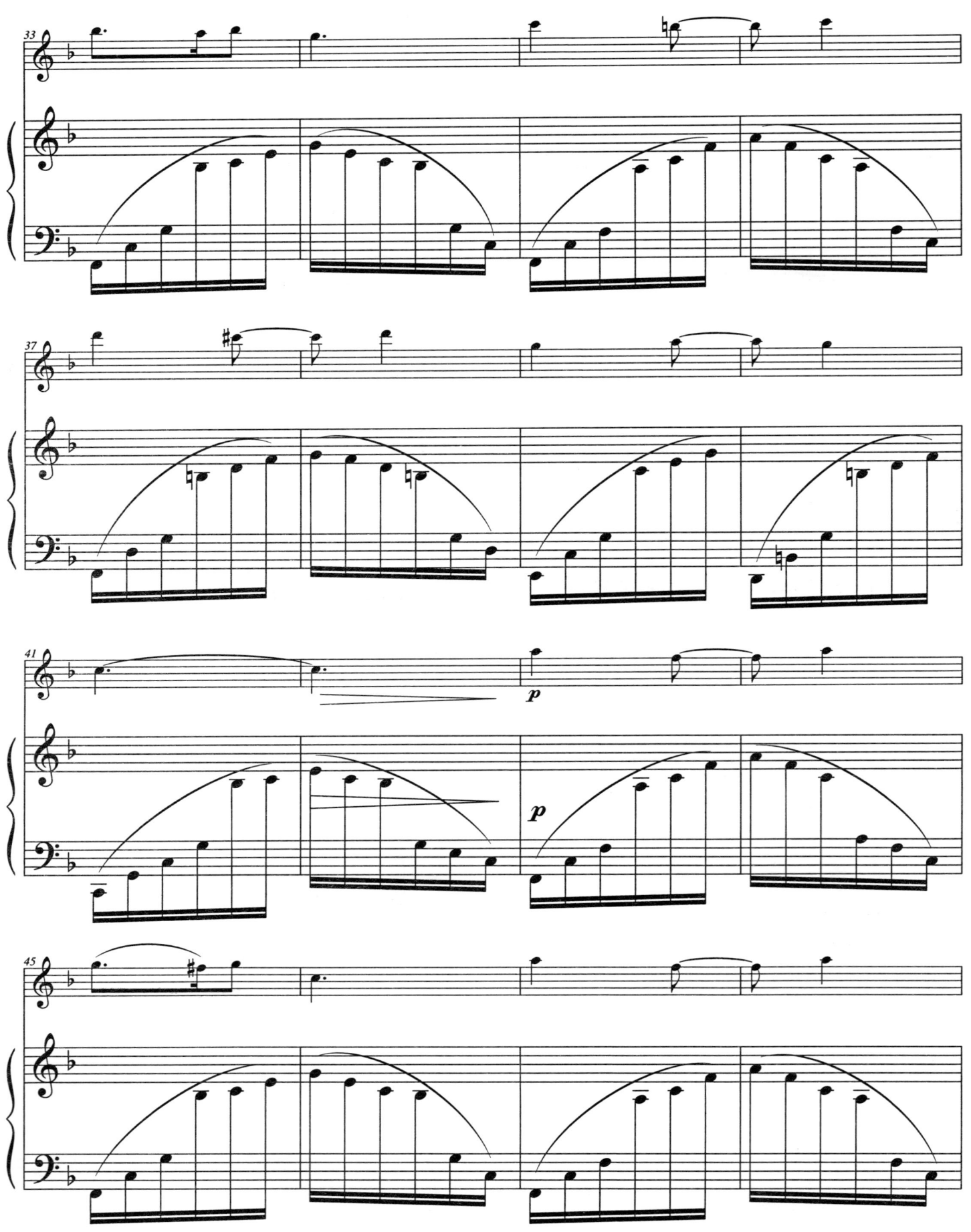

Paws for Thought

Gone Fishin'

Colin Cowles

Gone Fishin'

Gone Fishin'

Cat-Astrophe

Colin Cowles

Cat-Astrophe

Cat-Astrophe

Cat-Astrophe

Cat-Astrophe

Cats' Eyes

Colin Cowles

Cats' Eyes

Cats' Eyes

Vorwort

Als Katzenliebhaber kam Colin Cowles nicht umhin, eine Reihe von fantasievollen Stücken über unsere „pelzigen Freunde" zu komponieren. Seine eigenen Katzen – Puss, Boo und Olli – waren über etwa dreißig Jahre hinweg vollwertige Mitglieder der Familie. Diese kurzen, deskriptiven Stücke enthalten kleine Herausforderungen in technischer und musikalischer Hinsicht und stellen somit das ideale Unterrichts- und Spielmaterial im mittleren Schwierigkeitsgrad dar. Mit viel Sinn für Humor gespielt, wird den einzelnen Katzen Leben eingehaucht!

Colin Cowles

Colin Cowles begann seine Laufbahn als Musikerzieher. Er arbeitete zunächst als Schullehrer, bis ihm bewusst wurde, dass das Komponieren für ihn zunehmend wichtiger wurde. Er verließ daraufhin den Schuldienst und wurde freischaffender Pädagoge, um mehr Zeit für eigene Kompositionen zu haben. Besonders zahlreich sind seine Werke für Schüler im Anfängerstadium. Insgesamt umfassen seine Kompositionen eine große Bandbreite verschiedener Stile, Instrumente und Schwierigkeitsgrade. In vielen Kompositionen hat sich sein ausgeprägter Sinn für Humor niedergeschlagen, weswegen sie bei Schülern und Lehrern gleich gut ankommen. Allerdings haben selbst die ganz leicht und witzig wirkenden Stücke einen pädagogischen Hintergrund und ermöglichen so die Verbindung von Spaß und Lernerfolg.

Introduction

Il était prévisible que Colin Cowles, un amoureux des chats, compose une série de pièces originales qui leur est consacrée. Puss, Boo et Olli, ses trois chats, ont été des membres de la famille à part entière pendant près de trente ans. Ces petites pièces imagées sont d'un niveau technique et musical tout à fait abordable et en font un support d'enseignement et de jeu tout à fait adapté à des musiciens de niveau intermédiaire. Jouez avec humour et donnez vie à chacun des chats !

Colin Cowles

Colin Cowles a consacré l'essentiel de sa carrière à l'enseignement de la musique. Il débute en tant que professeur des écoles mais prend rapidement conscience qu'il souhaite accorder une place plus importante à la composition. Il quitte le milieu scolaire pour devenir professeur intervenant, une orientation qui lui permet de consacrer plus de temps à la composition. Il a composé de nombreuses pièces pour les musiciens débutants. Sa musique couvre un vaste registre de styles, d'instruments et de niveaux de difficulté. Son sens de l'humour, apparent dans beaucoup de ses compositions, est apprécié des professeurs comme des élèves mais ses pièces, y compris les plus légères, contiennent toutes en filigrane des objectifs pédagogiques précis, combinant l'aspect ludique et l'apprentissage.

Introductie

Voor kattenliefhebber Colin Cowles stond het onherroepelijk vast dat hij ooit een verzameling creatieve stukken over onze spinnende huisgenoten zou schrijven. Zijn eigen katten, Puss, Boo en Olli, waren voorname gezinsleden over een periode van zo'n dertig jaar. Deze korte beschrijvende stukken vormen in technisch en muzikaal opzicht een bescheiden uitdaging – als zodanig zijn ze uitstekend geschikt als lesmateriaal én voor optredens van enigszins gevorderde spelers. Breng met gevoel voor humor de verschillende katten tot leven!

Colin Cowles

Colin Cowles heeft zijn carrière voor een belangrijk deel gewijd aan het muziekonderwijs. Aanvankelijk werkte hij op scholen, maar hij realiseerde zich dat componeren steeds voornamer voor hem werd. Hij werd freelance docent, zodat hij tijd had om zich te concentreren op het componeren. Hij heeft een schat aan stukken geschreven voor beginnende musici. Zijn composities omvatten diverse stijlen, instrumenten en uitvoeringsniveaus. Zijn gevoel voor humor, doorklinkend in veel van zijn muziek, spreekt zowel docenten als leerlingen aan, hoewel zelfs zijn meest lichtvoetige werken een onderliggende ernst in zich hebben en plezier combineren met leren.

Colin Cowles

TASTY TUNES

CD Included

Tasty Tunes – short repertoire or concert pieces for the developing instrumentalist. The descriptive titles help conjure the mood of the music and act as a stimulus for the performer. With a mixture of styles and tempi these pieces represent a worthwhile challenge for players of grades three to five standard. Pieces may be performed individually or combined in any number of ways to create a suite – or perhaps a sweet? Although the music is approachable and light in character, it provides important and technical musical experience.

Enjoy playing and whet your audience's appetite.

Available for:
Flute	F 877-400
Clarinet	F 878-400
Alto Saxophone	F 879-400

Colin Cowles

POWER UP!

CD Included

Power Up! – ten short entertaining pieces in a variety of styles for solo instrument and piano. The structured technical and musical challenges make these pieces ideal for the developing instrumentalist of around grade three to five standard, or simply as short concert items.
The CD provided includes both demo and accompaniment tracks on an acoustic grand piano. It is particularly useful for home practice or for those instrumentalists who do not have an accompanist.

Available for:
Flute	F 861-400
Clarinet	F 862-400
Alto Saxophone	F 863-400